This book belongs to:

....

AUTUMN
PUBLISHING

Published in 2020
First published in the UK by Autumn Publishing
An imprint of Igloo Books Ltd
Cottage Farm, NN6 0BJ, UK
Owned by Bonnier Books
Sveavägen 56, Stockholm, Sweden
www.autumnpublishing.co.uk

1120 002
2 4 6 8 10 9 7 5 3 1
ISBN 978-1-83903-072-7

Illustrated by Gina Maldonado
Written by Suzanne Fossey

Designed by Lee Italiano
Edited by Suzanne Fossey

Printed and manufactured in China

Little
CHiCK

AUTUMN
PUBLISHING

I started in a cosy egg, all snug and warm within.

I tapped and pecked and made a hole. The light came shining in.

At last, the eggshell cracked in two. I wiggled my way free.
"Hello there, my Little Chick!"
my mummy said to me.

"You must be hungry," Daddy said.
"We'll bring you food to eat."
He came back with a wiggly worm.
Oh, what a lovely treat!

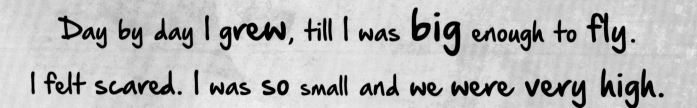

Day by day I grew, till I was **big** enough to fly.
I felt scared. I was **so** small and we were **very high.**

"**Help**," I cried.
"**I'm falling!**"

"Just flap your wings,"
said Dad.

I tried it and I soared up!
I felt so very glad.

My feathers touched the tops of trees as I **flew** across the sky.

Everything looks **very** tiny when you're flying up so high.

Not long after,
Mummy said, "The leaves
have begun to fall.
We're going on a journey,
now that you're no
longer small."

"We're flying somewhere warm for winter. It's really for the best.

"So shake your tail and flap your wings. It's time to leave the nest."

We joined a hundred other birds and soared across the sea.

For miles and miles
we flew and flew,
far from our cosy tree.

The city was too noisy...

... and the forest was too still.

"But this waterfall is perfect!"
I chirruped with a trill.

For months we stayed down in
the south, till I was fully grown.
Then springtime came around again.
It was time to fly back home.

Along the way, I met a friend.
We made a lovely pair!

We built a nest together, a home for us to share.

It wasn't long before I laid
five eggs, all smooth and round.
I kept them warm and snuggly,
high above the ground.

One day, I heard some noises: little **cracks** and **cricks.** **My eggs were hatching!** And out came five fluffy, little...

...chicks!

Bluebird chicks hatch
from their eggs in spring.
They stay in the nest and their
parents bring them food until they learn
to fly. When autumn comes, bluebirds fly south
to warmer places with hundreds of other birds, in
a journey called migration. They spend the winter
safe from cold weather and fly back north in
the spring to build their nests. The female
bluebirds lay eggs and keep them
warm by sitting on them until
they are ready to hatch.